JOE WICKS

THE BURPEE BEARS

A CHRISTMAS ADVENTURE

*I dedicate this book to Indie, Marley and the little baby
we are yet to meet in Rosie's tummy. We can't wait to
meet you and sit and enjoy this story together.
Love you always, Daddy
J. W.*

First published in hardback in the United Kingdom by HarperCollins *Children's Books* in 2022

HarperCollins *Children's Books* is a division of HarperCollins*Publishers* Ltd
1 London Bridge Street, London SE1 9GF

www.harpercollins.co.uk

HarperCollins*Publishers*
1st Floor, Watermarque Building, Ringsend Road, Dublin 4, Ireland

1 3 5 7 9 10 8 6 4 2

The Burpee Bears concept copyright © Joe Wicks 2021
Text copyright © Joe Wicks 2022
Illustrations copyright © Paul Howard 2022
Food and nutrition consultant: Charlotte Stirling-Reed

Hardback ISBN: 978-0-00-851671-0
Special edition ISBN: 978-0-00-859672-9

Printed in Italy

The tried-and-tested recipes in this book have been reviewed by a leading child nutritionist and carefully selected to suit most adults and children, but neither the publisher nor contributors can be held responsible for any adverse reaction to any of the ingredients. When using kitchen appliances you must always follow the manufacturer's instructions. Always allow hot liquids to cool before handling or blending. All exercises should be undertaken with adult supervision and due care. The exercises in this book have been carefully selected to benefit most adults and children, but neither the publisher nor contributors can be held responsible for any injuries related to these or similar physical activities.

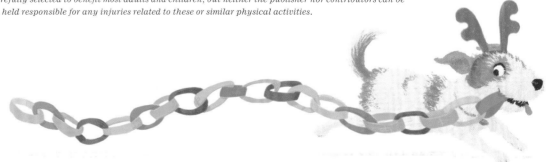

JOE WICKS
THE BURPEE BEARS
A CHRISTMAS ADVENTURE

Story co-written with **Vivian French**

Illustrated by **Paul Howard**

HarperCollins *Children's Books*

Snow is falling
over the **Burpee Bears'** house . . .

"Will it still be snowy on Christmas Day?"
Frankie asks. "When Granny Bear comes?"

"We'll have to wait and see,"
Mummy Bear tells him.

Bella does a twirl. "How long
do we have to wait?"

"Not too long. Let's fill the time
with fun!" says Daddy Bear,
and the three little bears bounce
with excitement.

"ARE WE READY?

ARE WE STEADY?

ARE WE PUTTING ON OUR WELLIES?"

Daddy Bear pulls on his hat.
"Let's build a snow bear!"

"ARE WE READY?
ARE WE STEADY?
LET'S GET BUILDING!"

"This will make us
big and strong,"
says Frankie,
as he scoops up
armfuls of snow.

"Peek-a-boo!"
says Baby Bear.

"Let's make snow angels," says Frankie.
"Arms up! Arms down! Flap those wings, little angel bears!"

"Flip flap!"

shouts Bella.

"Flip flap!"

"Wismass now?" asks Baby Bear.
"Not quite, Baby," Mummy Bear tells him.
"One day closer to Christmas," says Bella,
"and it's still snowing!"

At last it's Christmas Eve. The bears go ice-skating.

Swish, swish!

Swoosh, swoosh!

Swish, swish!

The bears whirl and twirl round the rink.

"Only **one** more sleep until we see Granny!" says Frankie.
"And it's STILL snowing."

The little bears go to bed early.

Bella gets treats ready for
Santa Bear and his reindeer.

Frankie snuggles

up in bed . . .

. . . and it's STILL snowing.

"Santy! Santy!"

squeals Baby Bear.

Daddy Bear tucks up Baby Bear with a kiss. "Santa Bear is busy delivering presents."

"ARE WE READY?"

"ARE WE STEADY?"

"ARE WE ALL SET FOR CHRISTMAS DAY?"

The three little bears hurtle into
Mummy and Daddy Bear's bedroom.

"What time is it?" Mummy yawns.

"Santy!" Baby Bear claps his paws.
"There's lots of snow," Frankie says.
"Lots and lots and LOTS!"

"Come and see!" Bella says.

"You're right," Mummy Bear says. "Oh dear! I don't think
Granny Bear will be able to get here…"

"We can't have Christmas without her!"
says Bella sadly.

"We NEED Granny Bear!"
says Frankie.

"ARE WE READY?
ARE WE STEADY?
IT'S TIME TO MAKE A PLAN!"

Daddy Bear jumps out of bed.

"If Granny Bear can't come to our house,
we'll take Christmas to her!"

"Let's make a list," says Bella at breakfast.

Mummy Bear grabs a pencil and paper. "Perfect!"

"We can use my sledge," says Frankie.

"Great idea," Daddy Bear tells him.

The bears load up
Frankie's sledge.

"Presents!"
says Bella.

"Check!"

"Lunch!" says
Daddy Bear, and
he fetches the
picnic basket.

"Potatoes!"

"Cranberry jelly!"

"Brussels sprouts!"

"YUCKY!"

"But Granny really
loves them . . .

Carrots!"

"Christmas pudding!"

"YUMMY trifle . . ."

"Oranges!"

"Ozzie!" says Frankie.

"Tree!" says Bella.

"Santy!"

"Check!"

"Let's put on our coats and hats and wellies! It's time to go!" And Mummy Bear opens the door. **WhoooOOOOooosh!** A flurry of snow blows in.

"Ooooh!" Frankie shivers. "It's FREEZING! Can we have Christmas **here** after all?"

"Granny would be ever so lonely," Bella tells him. Frankie pulls his hat down over his ears. "I want to see Granny," he says.

"Everybody set?" Daddy Bear picks up the rope that pulls the sledge.

"ARE WE READY?

ARE WE STEADY?

LET'S GET MOVING!"

STOMP! STOMP! STOMP! Past the snow bears . . .

TRAMP! TRAMP! TRAMP! Wave to the neighbours . . .

The snow is getting deeper.

"ARE WE READY?
ARE WE STEADY?
LET'S DO HIGH KNEES THROUGH THE SNOW . . .
. . . RIGHT TO THE TOP OF THE HILL!"

says Daddy Bear, and Frankie laughs.

CRUNCH! CRUNCH! CRUNCH! Past the snow angels . . .

STOMP! STOMP! STOMP!

Stomp to the top of the hill . . .

"Well done, guys," says Mummy Bear. "All aboard the sledge. Let's ZOOM down the hill!"

"ARE WE READY?"

"ARE WE STEADY?"

"LET'S GET ZOOMING!"

Daddy Bear gives the sledge a push,
then jumps on the end . . .
Away they go!

"Wheeeeeeeee!"

"We're flying!"

"Santy!"

The sledge
goes faster
and faster . . .

and FASTER
until . . .

. . . WHOOPS!

The sledge tips over
and presents scatter everywhere.

Baby Bear claps his paws.
"Santy!" he says. "Santy!"

Mummy and Daddy Bear head off
to pick up presents . . .

. . . just as the reindeer turn to land beside
the overturned sledge.

"**WOW!**" Bella and Frankie rub their eyes.

"**Ho! Ho! Ho!**" says Santa Bear.
"Looks like you could do with a helping hand!
Good thing I was held up by the snowstorm!"

The little bears help
Santa pile things back
on the sledge. Baby Bear
feeds carrots to the reindeer.
He offers them some sprouts.

"'Prouts?"

But the reindeer shake
their heads.

Santa **winks** at Baby Bear and lifts him on top of the parcels.

"Happy Christmas," he says.

"**Five** . . . **four** . . . **three** . . . **two** . . . **ONE!**"

shout the little bears, and Santa swoops up
into the sky, waving as he flies away.

"WOW!" says Daddy Bear, as he and Mummy come back with armfuls
of the presents. "Well done, guys! I'm proud of you for helping!"
Off they go to Granny's house . . .

. . . "SURPRISE!"

"Oh my goodness! This is the **best** Christmas ever!"
laughs Granny Bear, as the three little bears dance round her.

"We saw Santy Bear!" sings Baby Bear.
"We saw Santy!"

"I think you must have been dreaming, dear," says Granny Bear.
Then Baby Bear hands her a parcel . . .

"For Granny Bear. Love from, Santa Bear," she reads.

. . . And it's a **star** for the top of her tree.

HAPPY CHRISTMAS,
Burpee Bears!

WINTER WARM UP!

Are you ready? Are you steady? Let's get going!

Warm up on a cold day with this fun routine. It doesn't matter how many times you do it – just enjoy! Start with three times in a row and build up to five.

1 TWISTS

Stand up straight with your feet shoulder-width apart. Lift your arms to your chest, with elbows bent. Then slowly twist your body from left to right, without moving your legs. And repeat!

2 TOE TOUCHES

Stand up straight and stretch out your arms at shoulder height. Keeping your arms straight, bend to touch your right foot with your left hand. Stand up again and do the same on the other side.

3

SUPER-SLOW SQUATS

Stand up straight with your feet wide apart. Hold your arms straight out in front of your chest. Slowly bend your knees, keeping your back straight.

4

REVERSE LUNGE

Stand up straight, then take a big step back on your left foot. Keeping your back straight, bend your right knee and drop down until your left knee almost touches the ground. Stand up again and repeat on the other side.

5

HIGH FIVE
FOR THE WIN!

Well done! You are warmed up and ready for the day. Give each other a high five!

CALM YOUR MIND!

Are you ready for this relaxing routine? You can do the whole routine as many times as you like. It may help calm your mind and bring you happy thoughts. Try to keep breathing slowly as you go through the steps.

1

MOUNTAIN POSE TO FORWARD FOLD

Stand tall with your arms by your sides, then reach your arms up high before folding down to touch the ground.

PLANK TO LUNGE

2

Place your hands on the ground and form a plank. Then step your right leg forward into a low lunge. Return the leg back to the start and repeat with the left leg. In the plank keep your tummy tucked in and your back straight.

PLANK TO MOUNTAIN POSE

3

From your plank position gently walk your hands back to meet your feet. Take a moment in a forward fold before standing tall again.

4

AND RELAX!

When you are finished, take a tiny moment to wind down your body and say goodbye to the day.

FUN RECIPES WITH THE BURPEE BEARS

Safety in the Kitchen

*Before starting work, wash everyone's hands thoroughly. Children **must always have** a grown-up to help them in the kitchen, and should never use sharp knives, a food processor or handle anything hot. Never leave a pan on the heat unattended and always take care when putting things in or taking things out of the oven.*

ALWAYS check for allergies before you start on your ingredients!

FESTIVE GINGERBREAD BISCUITS

Makes 32 biscuits, or so, depending on your cookie shapes!

Plan your biscuit designs while your cookie dough is in the fridge!

INGREDIENTS

600g wholemeal flour

2 tsp ground cinnamon

2 tsp ground ginger

1½ tsp bicarbonate of soda

1 tsp sea salt

225g butter, softened

160ml honey

160ml black treacle

1 egg, beaten

a handful of raisins

METHOD

1. Mix together the dry ingredients and set aside.

2. Whisk the butter until fluffy. Add the honey and treacle, then the egg. Mix together. Then add the dry ingredients to make a dough.

3. Roll the dough into a ball and wrap in greaseproof paper before chilling in the fridge for an hour.

4. Pre-heat the oven to 190°C/170°fan/gas 5. Roll out dough on a lightly floured surface to 5mm thick. Cut out shapes with cookie cutters, then place them on a baking tray. Add raisins to decorate.

5. Bake for 10 to 15 minutes.

BERRY BLAST SMOOTHIE!

Makes 1 serving

TIP
How about adding a handful of spinach?

TIP
Freeze banana slices and berries the night before!

INGREDIENTS

1 banana, sliced and frozen

150g mixed berries, frozen

250ml milk (dairy or non dairy)

1 tsp vanilla extract

METHOD

1. Place all the ingredients in a blender. (If your fruit isn't frozen, use half the amount of milk plus a handful of ice cubes.)

2. Blend until smooth.

3. Pour into a glass or bowl and enjoy!

SNOW BEAR PIZZA

Makes 1 pizza, which should feed two small bears or one hungry bear!

INGREDIENTS

70g self-raising flour

¼ tsp baking powder

70g natural yoghurt

50ml passata

50g grated mozzarella

1 small mushroom, sliced

2 large pitted black olives

TIP
Lovely with salad!

METHOD

1. Heat oven to 240°C/220°C fan/gas 9.

2. Mix together the dry ingredients.

3. Mix in the yoghurt and use your hands to form a dough.

4. Shape the dough into a ball. Then, on a floured surface, roll into a rough circle, about 5mm thick.

5. Heat a dry frying pan, on medium/high. Add the pizza base and heat for 2 minutes on each side. Remove from pan.

6. Spread the passata over the pizza base, then evenly sprinkle mozzarella on top.

7. Add 2 mushroom slices for ears, 2 black olive halves for eyes, the end slice of a mushroom for a nose and 3 thin black-olive slices for a mouth.

8. Place the pizza on a baking tray and cook for 10 minutes, then serve!

A Note from Joe

I really hope that you have all enjoyed this festive adventure with the Burpee Bears. They are a busy family, but they know just how much fun it can be to spend time together during the holiday season. Sharing mealtimes is one of my favourite things in the world to do with my family, and I love to share the wonder of stories and books with my children.

I hope you'll feel inspired by my story to go on your own Burpee Bear adventures whatever the weather. Do have fun joining in the exercises at the end. Keep moving! Just a few small changes will make a difference. Let's make every day a healthy and happy one!

And finally, thank you to all of you for reading my book.
I hope you keep going with the Burpee Bears . . .
There are even more adventures to come!

Lots of love,

Joe

P.S.
Bella Bear wants to show you how to do a burpee . . . here's how!